# Flash's Day at the Park

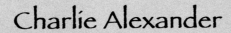

Charlie Alexander

# Flash's Day at the Park

*By Charlie Alexander*

# Flash's Day
# at the Park

## Written by Charlie ALexander
## Art work by Charlie ALexander

# Flash arrives at the Park.

## It sure looks like fun.

# Flash was anxious to try the Dodge Cars.

Crash and bump was so much fun!

# Flash walked very quickly.

He wanted to ride the
Roller Coaster!

It was very high and
very fast!

Flash loved it!

# Now it was time for the Ferris Wheel.

A nice calm ride. Flash could see the whole Park!

# "Oh boy!" barked Flash.

He was very happy to have some popcorn.

# A thrilling slide was going to be next.

Flash thought about closing his eyes.

# The Merry-Go-Round
# wasn't nearly so scary!

Flash was having a blast.

Flash was a little nervous
to slide down the Tower.

But he wanted to ride it again!

# Flash loved riding up the Ski Lift!

"It is going to be exciting to try out these fancy skis," thought Flash.

Flash was happy to have
a ski pole.

The way down was fast and slippery!

# It's a good time for a hot dog!

Flash loved his delicious lunch.

# Playing toss the rings was right after lunch!

Flash was happy to win a prize for two nicely tossed rings.

# There was one more really cool ride to try.

It turned out to be a flight like never before!

# Miniature Golf was par for the course.

Flash really liked his new seven iron.

# The Haunted House was right around the corner!

Ghosts and Goblins and scary surprises.

# Flash was a little sad.

He missed the music that the band had played.

# It was time to dribble the basketball.

## Flash dunked his shot!

# Flash threw a fast ball!

# Strike three!

# Climbing the Wall was hard!

Flash's muscles were getting tired.

The water fountains made a lot of bubbles.

It was a chance to cool off.

# A high dive off the spring board.

Flash was good at doing a jackknife.

# Flash likes to swim.

He has a nice backstroke.

This train took Flash to see
the different animals.

The ride was a little bumpy.

Tall Giraffes and big grey Elephants
were smiling at Flash!

He smiled right back.

The Alligators were getting ready to eat lunch.

Flash was almost ready to sit and have a glass of orange juice too.

# Flash was having a Whale of a time.

He was surprised to see how beautiful the Whale looked!

"Wow!!" yelped Flash.

Fireworks lit up the sky!

# The Park was about to close.

Flash found the Exit and was thrilled with a wonderful day at the park!

The End

Flash spent the day riding Roller Coasters and Ferris Wheels. He enjoyed seeing Elephants and Giraffes. Playing Baseball and Basketball added to a delightful day! Flash thought the Fireworks were the perfect ending for a perfect day at the Park!

Charlie is a Jazz Pianist and author of eleven books He is busy writing a twelfth book. Charlie lives in Ocala Florida with his wife Becky and of course his pal Flash

To order additional copies of this book, contact:
Xlibris
844-714-8691
www.Xlibris.com
Orders@Xlibris.com

Library of Congress Control Number:  2023902001
ISBN:   Softcover              978-1-6698-6544-5
        Hardcover             978-1-6698-6545-2
        EBook                 978-1-6698-6543-8

Print information available on the last page

Rev. date: 04/13/2023

Printed in the United States
by Baker & Taylor Publisher Services